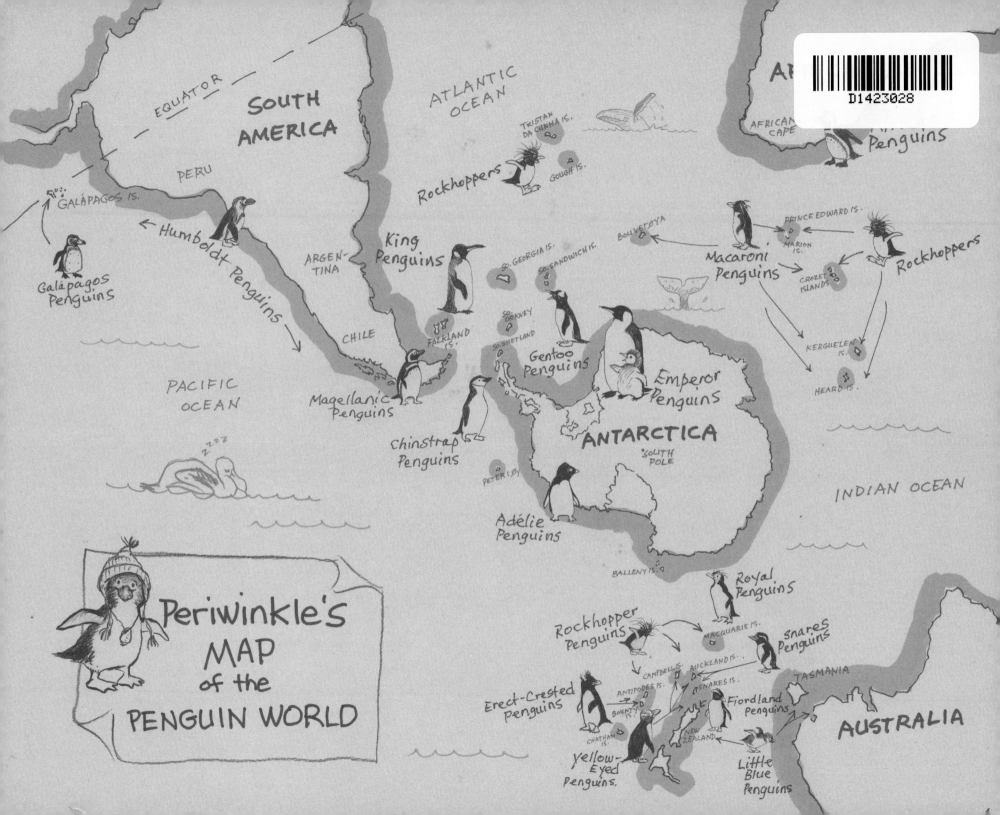

EQUATOR

SOUTH AMERICA

ATLANTIC OCEAN

AF

PERU

AFRICAN CAPE

Penguins

GALÁPAGOS IS.

TRISTAN DA CUNHA IS.

Rockhoppers

GOUGH IS.

← Humboldt Penguins →

Galápagos Penguins

King Penguins

ARGEN-TINA

BOUVETØYA

PRINCE EDWARD IS.

MARION IS.

Macaroni Penguins

Rockhoppers

CHILE

SO. GEORGIA IS.

SO. SANDWICH IS.

CROZET ISLANDS

FALKLAND IS.

SO. ORKNEY

KERGUELEN IS.

PACIFIC OCEAN

SO. SHETLAND

Gentoo Penguins

Emperor Penguins

HEARD IS.

Magellanic Penguins

Chinstrap Penguins

ANTARCTICA

SOUTH POLE

INDIAN OCEAN

PETER I. ØY

Adélie Penguins

BALLENY IS.

Royal Penguins

Rockhopper Penguins

MACQUARIE IS.

Snares Penguins

Periwinkle's MAP of the PENGUIN WORLD

CAMPBELL IS.

AUCKLAND IS.

TASMANIA

ANTIPODES IS.

SNARES IS.

Erect-Crested Penguins

BOUNTY IS.

Fiordland Penguins

AUSTRALIA

CHATHAM IS.

NEW ZEALAND

Yellow-Eyed Penguins

Little Blue Penguins

Blue Sneaker Press

Periwinkle's Journey was published by Blue
Sneaker Press. Blue Sneaker works with authors,
illustrators, nonprofit organizations, and
corporations to publish children's books that
engage, entertain, and educate kids on subjects
that affect our world. Blue Sneaker Press is
an imprint of Southwestern Publishing Group,
Inc., 2451 Atrium Way, Nashville, TN 37214.
Southwestern Publishing Group is a wholly owned
subsidiary of Southwestern/Great American, Inc.,
Nashville, Tennessee.

Southwestern Publishing Group, Inc.
www.swpublishinggroup.com • 800-358-0560

Christopher G. Capen, President
Carrie Hasler, Development Director,
   Blue Sneaker Press
Kristin Connelly, Managing Editor
Vicky Shea, Senior Art Director

Doug Schmitt, Art Director, Suzy's World

Periwinkle's Journey copyright © 2016 Suzy's
   World, LLC
Illustrations copyright © 2016 Suzy Spafford
Text copyright © 2016 Judy Petersen-Fleming

ISBN: 978-1-943198-03-0
Library of Congress Control Number: 2015956895
Printed in China
10 9 8 7 6 5 4 3 2 1

Periwinkle's Journey

Judy Petersen-Fleming and Suzy Spafford

Blue Sneaker Press

It was spring in Australia when Periwinkle, the little blue penguin, looked up. Albert Albatross had dropped a letter at her feet. "Special delivery!" he announced.

Periwinkle picked up the letter and ran to show her best friend, Petey Platypus.

"Petey," she shouted, "I got a letter! I got a letter!"

"Well, open it already!" he cried.

COME TO MY

Meet all of our 17

Kiana

Eddie

Jenny

Micky

Charlie

Ciera

Harry

Gus

Galápagos

Humboldt

Snares

Chinstrap

Gentoo

Macaroni

Adélie

King

WHERE: Antarctic Peninsula

WHEN: 2nd Full Moon This Summer

"It's a birthday party invitation from my cousin Crystal in Antarctica," said Periwinkle.

BIRTHDAY PARTY

Penguin Cousins!

SIGNED:

CRYSTAL

Maggie — Magellanic
Ruby — Royal
Yancy — Yellow-Eyed
Kerstyn — Erect-crested
Frankie — Fiordland
Cappy — African
Rocky — Rockhopper
This is you — Periwinkle — Little Blue

This is me; Crystal — Emperor
Mama

"Oh, look—there you are," said Petey. It was easy to find Periwinkle. She was the only blue penguin in the group.

Periwinkle grew quiet. "Gosh," she thought. "I'm different from the rest."

Later that day, Periwinkle showed the invitation to her mother. "But, Mama, they're all black-and-white and *bigger*."

Mama smiled at Periwinkle. "Now remember what I always say: *It's not how you look on the outside, it's what's inside that matters.*"

The next morning Petey came over to play. "Say, Petey, do you know where Antarctica is?" Periwinkle asked.

Petey didn't have a clue. "Let's go ask Mr. Wendell. He knows everything!"

Mr. Wendell was in his classroom when they arrived. "Here we are in Australia," he said pointing to the globe, "and Antarctica is way down at the bottom. It's all covered in ice and snow."

"Brrr," shivered Petey.

"Will there be *polar bears* down there?" asked Periwinkle.

"Don't worry," Mr. Wendell assured her. "Polar bears live only at the top of the earth, in the Arctic."

"Whew." Periwinkle was relieved but still a little scared.

The next day Albert was back. "Ahoy, Periwinkle. Meet Rocky Rockhopper from New Zealand!"

"Hellooo, Cousin!" called Rocky. "Ready to ride with me to Antarctica?"

"Did you say *ride*? Way up in the *sky*?"
Periwinkle's eyes opened wide.

"Sure!" said the albatross. "It's too far to
swim, and everyone knows penguins can't fly."

"You can do it, Periwinkle," assured Rocky.

Soon it was time for them to go.
"Periwinkle," Mama said, "I made you a hat
to help keep you warm." Then she slipped
a special necklace over Periwinkle's head.
"And this will remind you to be brave!"

Periwinkle touched the beautiful seashell.
"I feel braver already!" Periwinkle chirped.

Then Mama turned to Rocky. "You should wear a hat, too," she started.

"Oh, no, no, no!" he squealed, shaking his head. "We rockhoppers *never* wear hats. They just mess up our head feathers!"

Everyone laughed.

Periwinkle's heart beat fast as she climbed aboard Albert's swing. After giving hugs all around, she said good-bye to her warm-weather friends and family. Then Albert lifted off. Periwinkle held on tight.

"Now departing for Antarctica. Next stop, Cape Point, Africa!" Albert announced.

"*Africa*?" shouted Periwinkle and Rocky in surprise.

"Yep," Albert called down. "Your African cousin needs a ride, too."

They flew for days and days. Periwinkle often held the shell necklace from Mama, which reminded her to be brave. At night they rested on the ocean's surface. The waves rocked them to sleep.

At last Africa appeared below. Cousin Cappy was calling to them from the shoreline. "Hee-haw-hee-haw-*hi!*" Cappy said, sounding just like a donkey. "I thought you'd never get here!"

The three cousins made their way to
Cappy's rookery. Suddenly Cappy stopped.
Several Cape fur seals were sleeping.
"Shhh," she whispered. "The seals can
get *really* grumpy if we wake them up."

Cappy's home was filled with trinkets and treasures and piles and piles of rocks. What a collection she had!

Cappy showed them a beautiful sparkling diamond. "I'm giving *this* to Crystal for her birthday."

"Here is my present," replied Rocky. He held up a green jade stone from New Zealand.

Periwinkle gazed sadly at the pretty stones. "Oh no, I forgot to bring a gift."

"Don't worry," said Cappy. "You can give her this!"
She plucked a shiny blue stone from her collection and
tucked it into Periwinkle's backpack pocket. "It's blue,
just like your feathers," Cappy smiled.

Periwinkle cheered up. "Oh, thank you, Cappy!"

Night fell over Cape Point. A million stars sparkled
in the African sky. Albert settled on a nearby rock.
Cappy and Rocky were asleep too. But Periwinkle
was wide awake.

"I wish I were black-and-white, too," she thought.

Then, holding her seashell, Periwinkle remembered Mama's words: *It's not how you look on the outside that matters.* Periwinkle sighed. Soon she was fast asleep.

The next morning it was time to go. "Climb aboard and buckle up!" Albert announced.

But every time Albert tried to lift off, he couldn't get up in the air. Now that there were three penguins on the swing, it was just too heavy.

"What are we going to do?" cried Periwinkle.

"We'll figure out a way. Don't worry," said Albert. "Wait here—I'll be right back."

The cousins watched Albert fly out over the waves.

"Look! It's a pod of humpback whales on their way to Antarctica!" Cappy exclaimed.

When Albert flew back, he was all smiles. "The humpback whales will swim with you the rest of the way."

"Will you come, too?" Periwinkle hoped.

Albert shook his head. "No, I'll meet you in Antarctica."

The humpback whales were happy
to have the penguins' company. The
penguins swam fast, like little torpedoes.
The whales were amazed!

breeeeoup!

oouup!

weeeooooiuup!

brbrreeeee!

One morning Cappy heard whale sounds coming from the deep. "Listen," she said. "The whales are singing for us!"

The three penguins giggled as they swam and danced along to the song of the whales.

Then they heard loud honking from across the water. It was Crystal with some of the cousins. They were in Antarctica at last!

Periwinkle raced Rocky and Cappy for the icy shore. One, two, three, they popped onto the ice.

"Welcome to Antarctica!" Crystal honked as the others squawked loudly in greeting.

Giggling with excitement, the penguin cousins gathered together. One-by-one, they waddled up to a big map to show where they were from.

Then there was a pause. Crystal looked around. "Where is Galápagos Gus?"

"He couldn't find a ride," honked Harry the Humboldt penguin.

Everyone was a little sad.

Once everybody got settled, it was time for the party. "Let's play Follow-the-Penguin!" suggested Crystal. She led the penguins down the ice slide, shouting, "Wheee!" Periwinkle had never had so much fun.

Suddenly there was a loud cry overhead. "Waaait for meee!" Albert Albatross was carrying a special delivery.

Out tumbled a bundle, all wrapped up in scarves, flapping its flippers.

"Galápagos Gus! You made it after all!" cried Crystal.

"I would never miss your party," he exclaimed, wrapping a pink scarf around Crystal. "I thought you could use this. It's free-e-e-zing down here!" he honked.

After seeing the present from Galápagos Gus, each cousin presented Crystal with a special gift. Rocky's pretty green stone was a big hit.

Next it was Cappy's turn. Crystal's eyes lit up. "How bee-u-ti-ful! It sparkles, just like the ice we live on. Thank you, Cappy!"

Periwinkle went to look for the shiny blue stone for Crystal . . . but it was gone. "It must have fallen out on our long swim from Africa!" Periwinkle realized. "What should I do?"

Periwinkle was so sad. She didn't want to be the only cousin without a gift.

Then she thought of her shell necklace. But she loved it, and Mama had made it just for *her*. It had helped her be so brave.

Slowly, she took off the necklace and presented it to Crystal. "Happy birthday," Periwinkle said softly.

"For me?" asked Crystal. "I've never had such a special gift—and from such a special penguin!"

"You mean I'm *special?*" asked Periwinkle.
"But . . . I'm so different. I'm not black-and-
white like everyone else. I'm blue,"
she muttered.

"Why would you want to be like
everyone else?" Crystal asked.

Periwinkle looked around. One penguin had a chinstrap. Another one had stripes going in different directions. Someone else had yellow eyes. They were all different.

"You're right," replied Periwinkle. "I like my blue feathers. I like being small. I like being *me*!"

"Yes, Periwinkle," the penguins chimed in together. "Only you can be you!"

"Let's huddle together emperor-style now that we're all here at last," said Crystal. And they did, singing "Happy Birthday" to Crystal as the southern lights danced in the sky.

Periwinkle had never been so happy and proud to just be herself—a little blue penguin from Australia.

Acknowledgments

We are deeply grateful for the encouragement and support provided by so many people to bring *Periwinkle's Journey* to fruition.

To my daughters, Ciera Fleming and Kiana Fleming, thank you for being my inspiration to create this story in hopes that children and adults alike will be encouraged to connect and care more about nature. To Karen Petersen, who worked her magic as our first copy editor, and to Kendra Winhall, who provided such a wonderful kid perspective, thank you both. —Judy

To my husband, Ray, thank you for always believing in everything I do. To Doug Schmitt, what would I do without my immensely talented art director? Thank you for all you do to bring Suzy's World to life. And for the inspiration that I found in Frank S. Todd's *Birds & Mammals of the Antarctic, Subantarctic & Falkland Islands* and in Roger Tory Peterson's *Penguins*, thank you for your tremendous talents. —Suzy

Finally, both of us wish to thank Chris Capen for his vision that motivated us to create Suzy's World and his nurturing along the way. And a heartfelt thanks to Carrie Hasler for her passion and innovative ability to help us see through the eyes of a child.